P9-EDU-660

For Álvaro, my little birdie who
comes out with the sun.
And for my parents, because
growing old is a great feat.

Paula Merlán

To my true friends.

Sonja Wimmer

A Surprise for Mrs. Tortoise
Somos8 Series

www.nubeocho.com – info@nubeocho.com

Original title: *Una sorpresa para tortuga*
English translation: Ben Dawlatly and Kim Griffin
Text editing: Rebecca Packard

Distributed in the United States by
Consortium Book Sales & Distribution

First edition: 2017
ISBN: 978-84-946333-4-8

Printed in China by Asia Pacific Offset,
respecting international labor standards.

A Surprise for Mrs. Tortoise

Paula Merlán
Sonja Wimmer

nubeOCHO

The sun still hadn't risen, but Mrs. Tortoise was already awake. She popped her head out of her shell and had a look around.

Though everything was as it should be, she felt like something extraordinary was about to happen to her. Birdie, her very best friend, was still dreaming away in his nest.

Just like every morning, Mrs. Tortoise took very slow steps to a nearby pond to freshen up. But that morning, something startled her when she saw her own reflection in the water.

Her face was wrinkled and her shell looked worn out. It was right then that she felt old and very, very sad.

As the sun came up, Birdie came fluttering around.

"Good morning, my friend! What's wrong?"

"I feel really sad," replied Mrs. Tortoise. "Time goes by so fast... Look at me! I'm old and wrinkled! And don't even get me started on my shell. It's a disaster!"

Birdie took a good long look at her shell.

"You're right, it does need fixing up a little, but that's easy enough," he said confidently.

"I've got it! We'll ask the sky to lend you a handful of stars. Your shell will twinkle beautifully."

Mrs. Tortoise thought it sounded like a good idea. So the sky sent her some very pretty stars.

Her shell sparkled brightly, but when night came and it got dark, the light from the shiny stars wouldn't let her sleep.

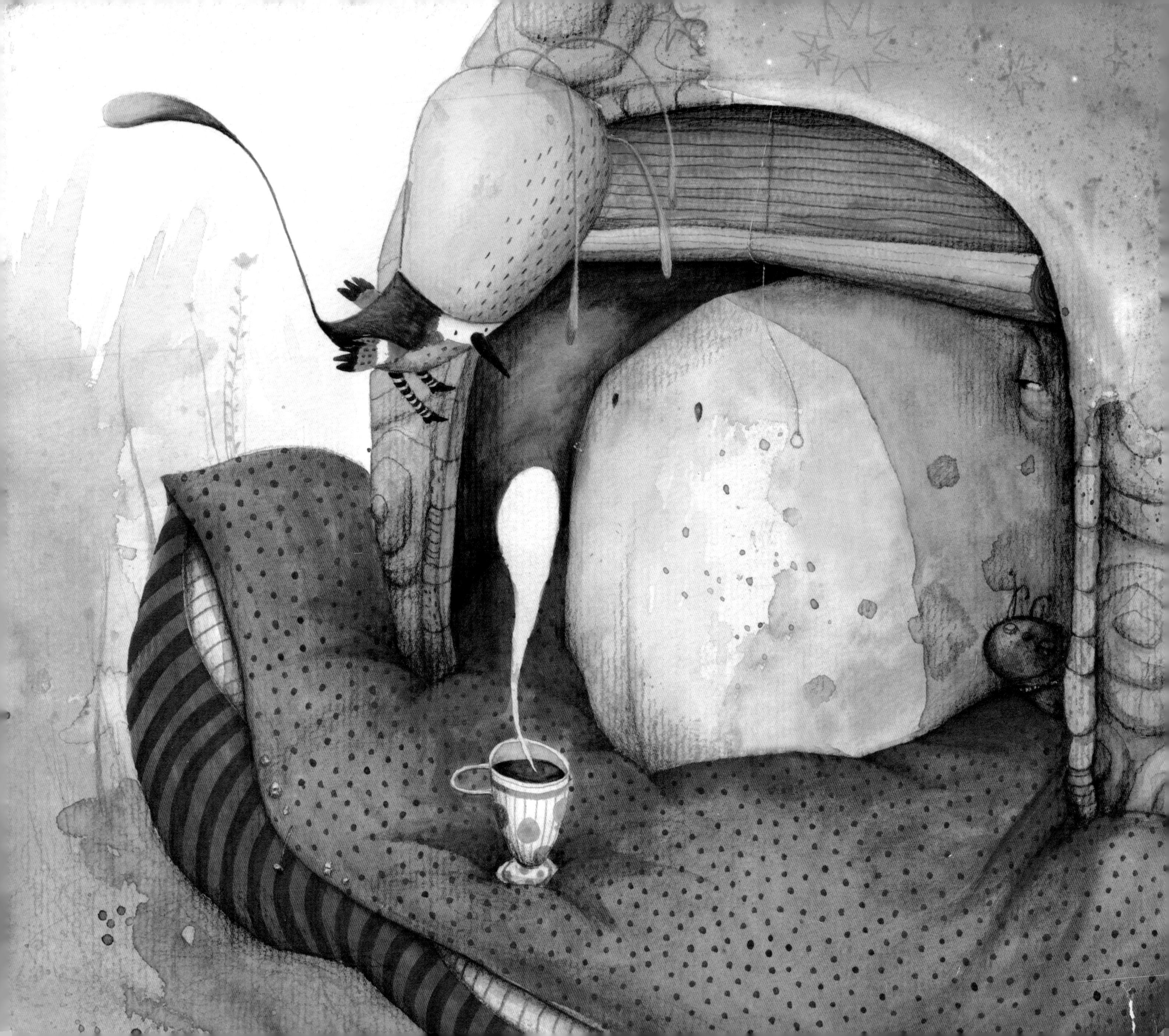

The next morning, Birdie flew over to see how his friend was doing. Mrs. Tortoise was very tired.

“My shell was so bright that I didn’t get any sleep at all,” she cried.

Birdie came up with another idea straightaway.

“I’ve got it! We’ll ask the plants to give us a bunch of flowers. That way you can cover your shell with beautiful colors.”

Mrs. Tortoise thought it would be a good idea. So the plants sent a sack full of flowers.

Mrs. Tortoise's shell was splashed all over with colors, but soon the petals got old and dry, and their sweet smell faded away.

“It’s no use,” said Mrs. Tortoise, disheartened.

"Don't be upset, my friend!" Birdie cried out. "We will ask the wind to sweep in some clouds. That way you will look just like a soft cotton ball."

Mrs. Tortoise thought it might be a good idea. So the wind came and gave Mrs. Tortoise a couple of clouds that completely enveloped her shell.

But soon the clouds made her feel wet and uncomfortable.

“It’s still no use,” Mrs. Tortoise cried desperately.

Birdie couldn’t think of any other way to help her.

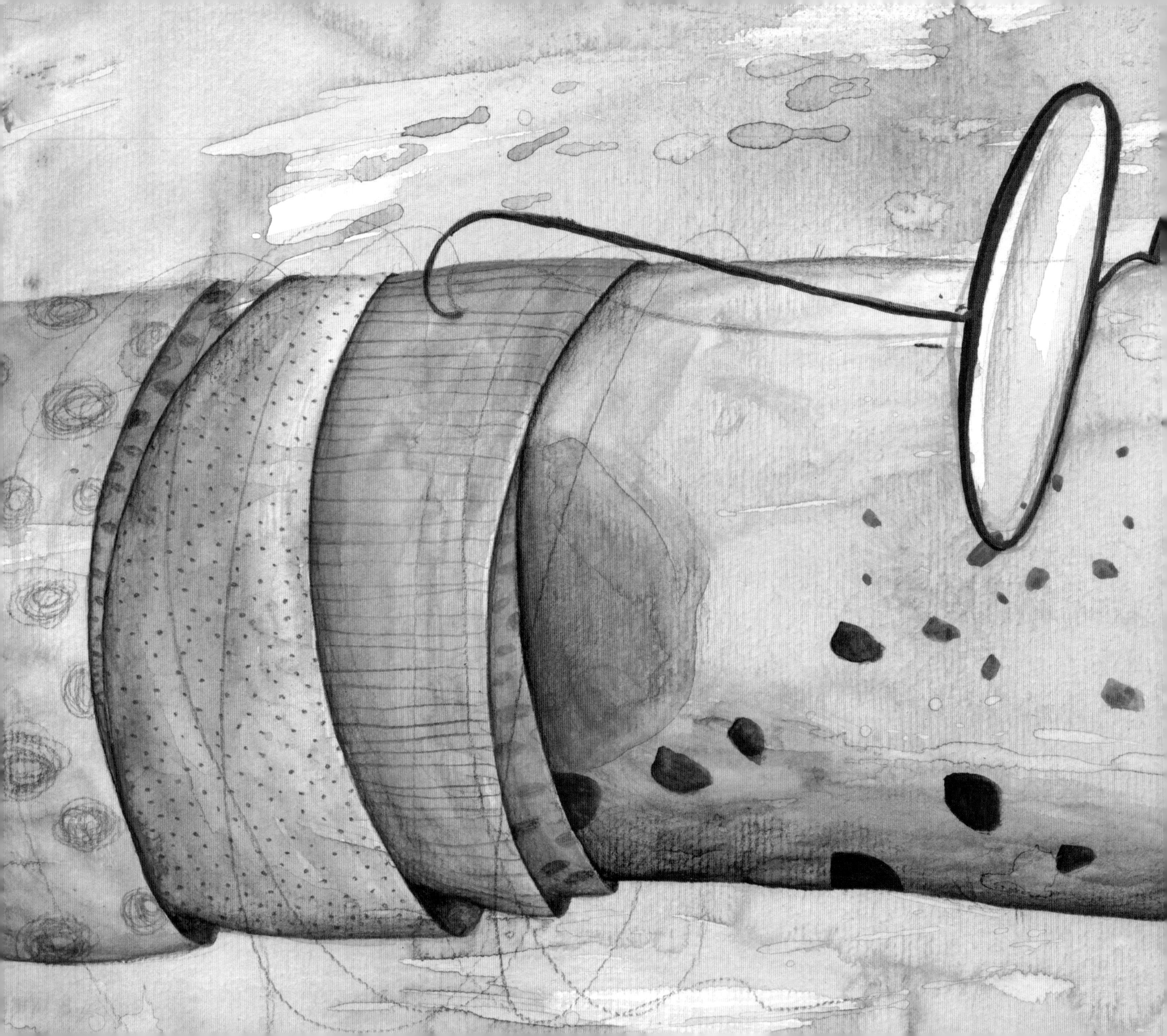

"Maybe, just maybe, if we ask..."

"I've had enough!" Mrs. Tortoise shouted. "All you've managed to do is make me feel worse."

Angry, Mrs. Tortoise disappeared into the woods. As she walked along, she started to cry.

She knew Birdie was only trying to help her, and she had been really mean to him. She stopped to rest a little while and fell fast asleep.

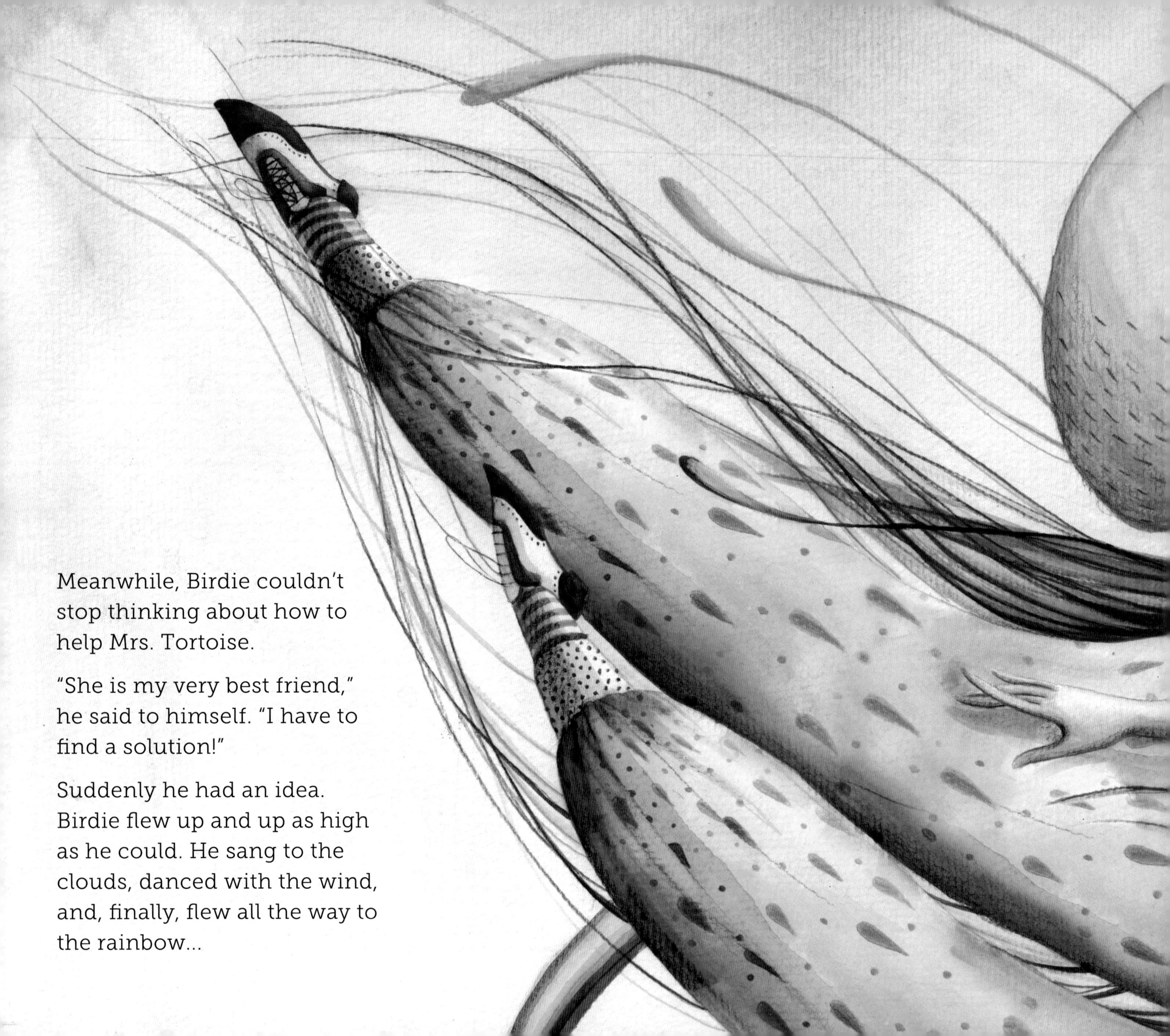

Meanwhile, Birdie couldn't stop thinking about how to help Mrs. Tortoise.

"She is my very best friend," he said to himself. "I have to find a solution!"

Suddenly he had an idea. Birdie flew up and up as high as he could. He sang to the clouds, danced with the wind, and, finally, flew all the way to the rainbow...

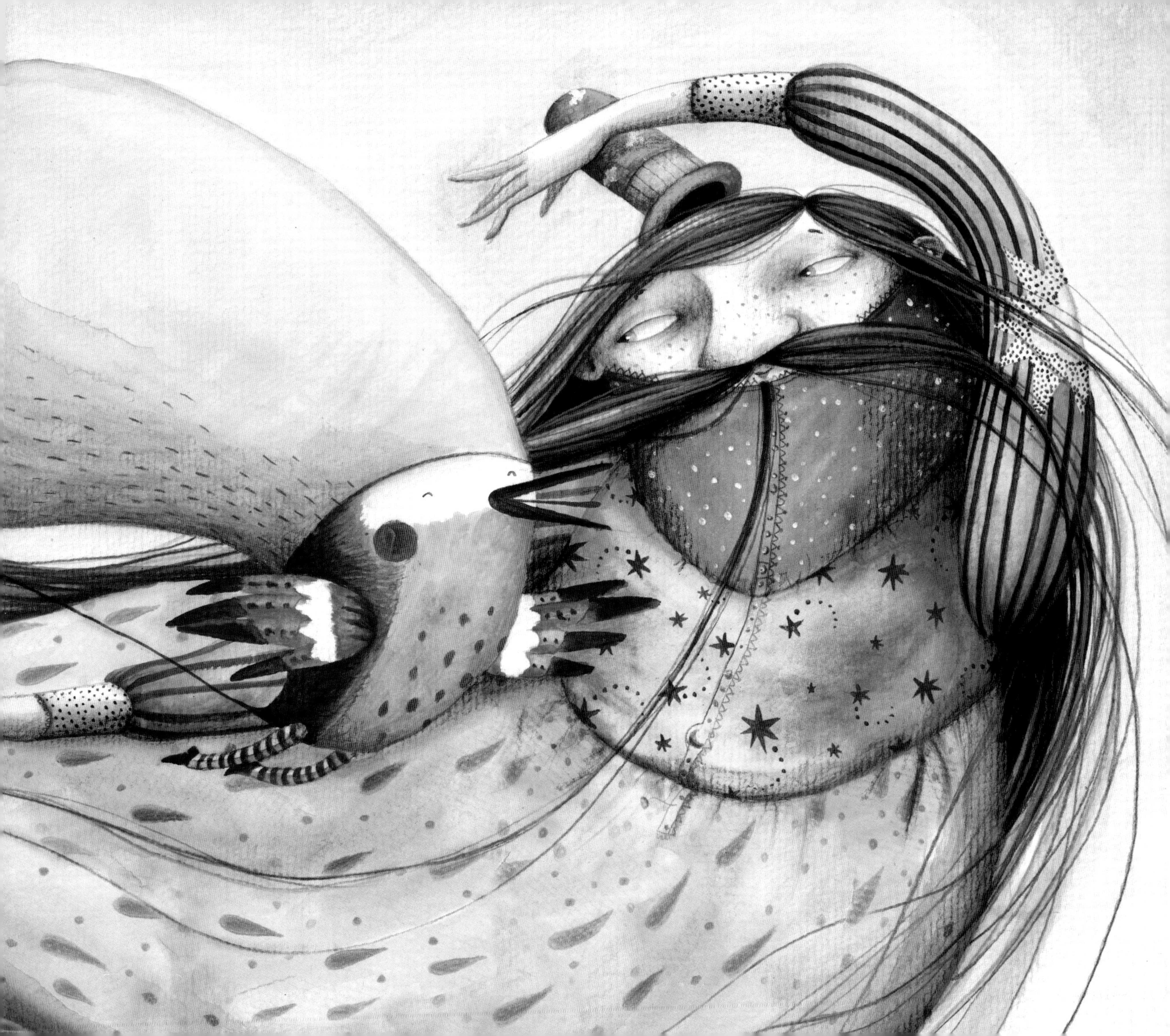

At sunrise, Mrs. Tortoise woke up to a surprise.

“Oh! I must have dozed off!” she exclaimed.

Just then, she noticed she was close to the pond where she always freshened up, and since she was feeling thirsty, she went over for a drink. She gazed at her reflection in the water.

"But... what's happened?" an astonished Mrs. Tortoise asked herself.

"Do you like it?" Birdie asked, nervously fluttering above his friend.

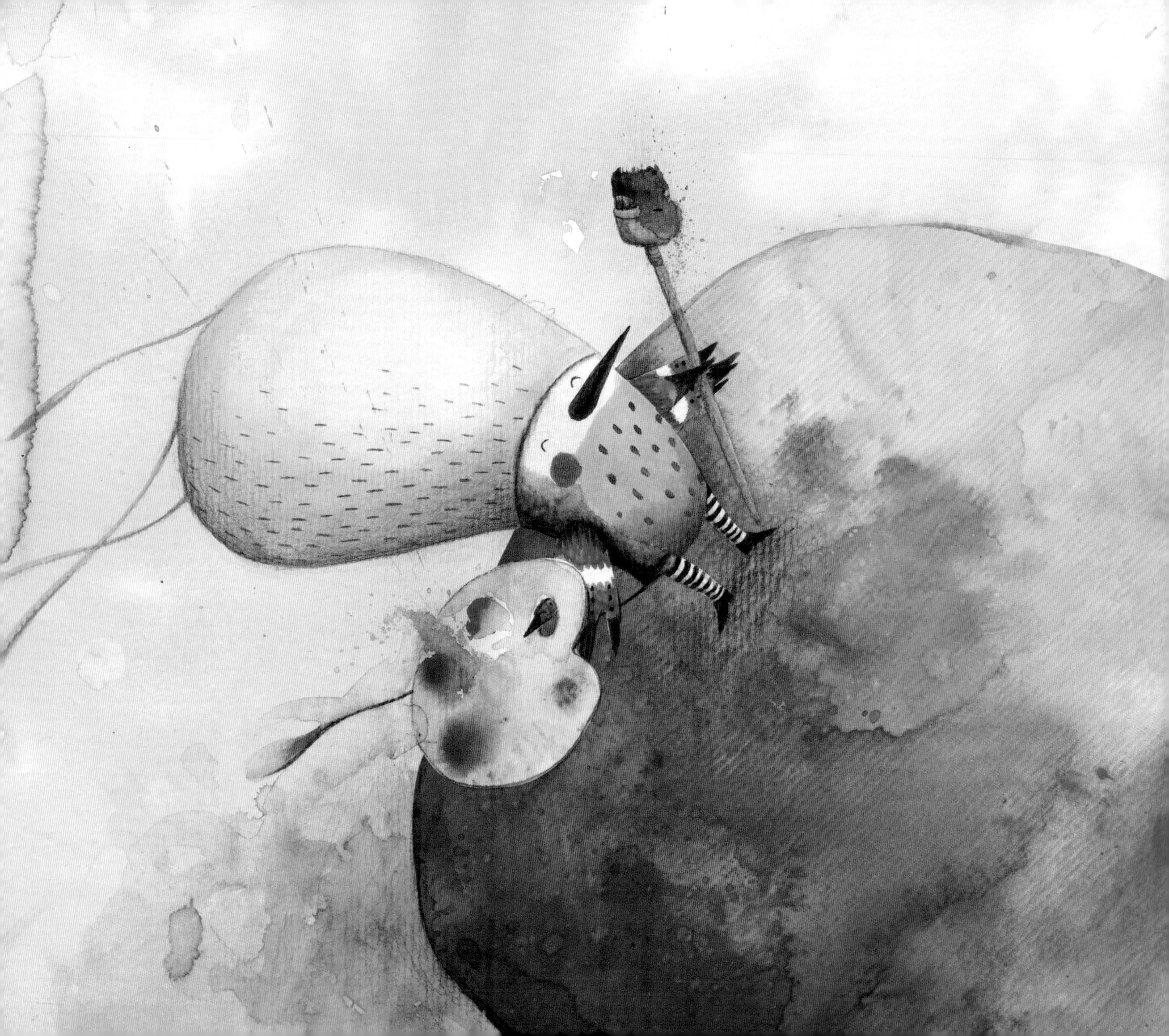

“It’s magnificent!” she said, admiring her colorful appearance.

“The rainbow gave me some paint and... well, there you have it. Besides singing, I also love to paint,” chirped Birdie.

"It's so pretty!" said the grateful Mrs. Tortoise. "Yesterday I was so mean to you. I hope you can forgive me. You know you are my very best friend, right?"

"You're my best friend too!" replied Birdie excitedly.

Mrs. Tortoise knew that something extraordinary was going to happen to her, and she was right.

The wrinkles on her face and her old shell didn't bother her anymore. Birdie was right by her side, and that was all that mattered.

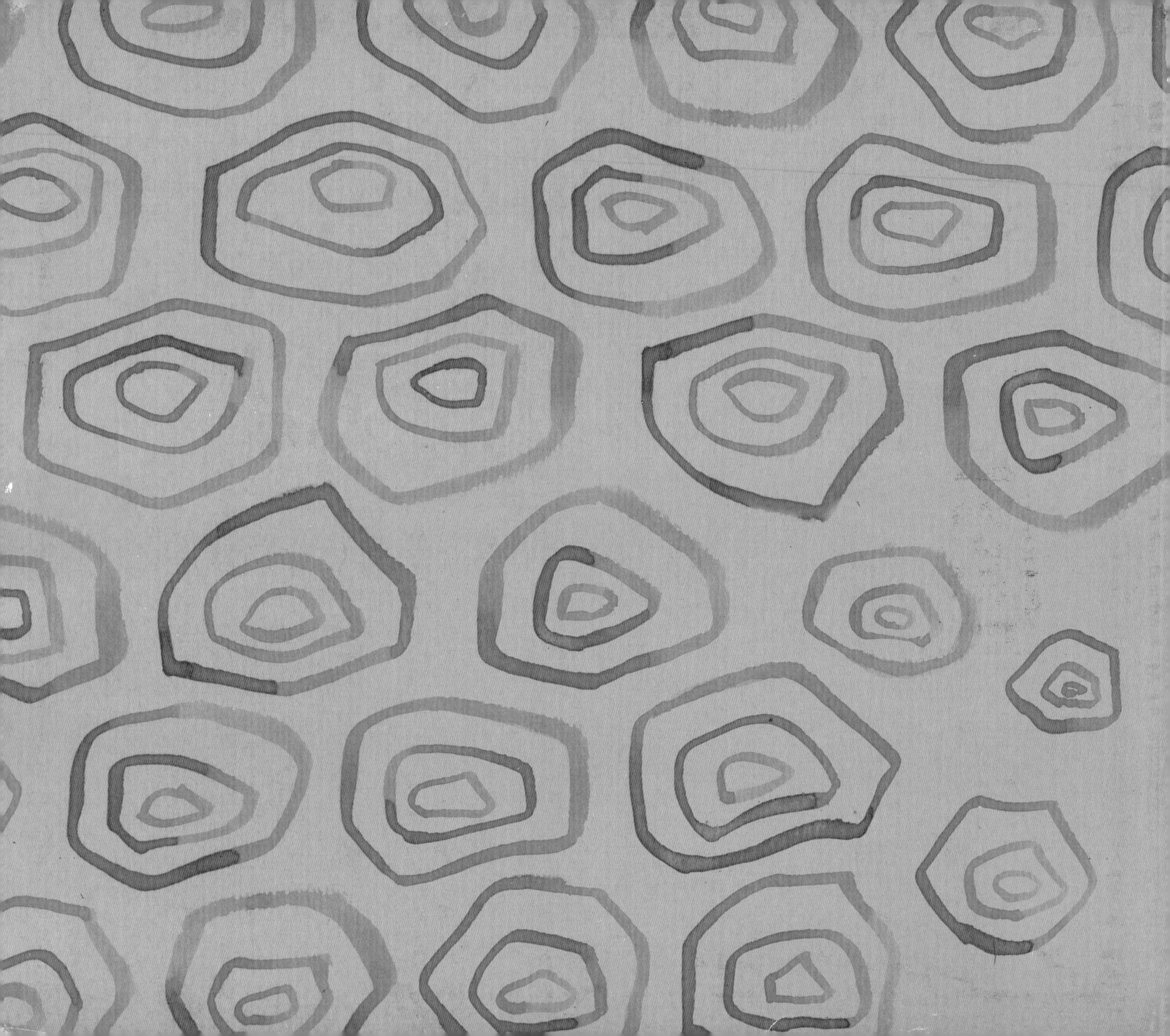

P9-EEK-347

For Michael my Superhero & anyone out in the cold.

First U.S. edition 2006

Library of Congress Cataloging-in-Publication Data is available.

Library of Congress Catalog Card Number 2004061849

ISBN 0-7636-2761-5

10 9 8 7 6 5 4 3 2 1

Printed in China

This book has been typeset in Godlike Emboldened
The illustrations were done in watercolor, ink, and pastel.

Candlewick Press
2067 Massachusetts Avenue
Cambridge, Massachusetts 02140

visit us at www.candlewick.com

Cold Paws, Warm Heart

Madeleine Floyd

CANDLEWICK PRESS
CAMBRIDGE, MASSACHUSETTS

Far away, in the land of snow and ice, lived a large polar bear who was always cold and all alone. His name was Cold Paws.

When he was young, Cold Paws tried to play with the other animals,

but he was too big for their games and no one wanted to play with him.

That's when he started
to feel cold inside.

Poor Cold Paws,
he was very lonely.
He sat alone and
shivered.

Time passed slowly for Cold Paws.
The only thing that kept him
company was a silver flute,
which he played each day to
forget his troubles.

In the land of snow and ice there also
lived a little girl named Hannah.
The people in her village said that no one lived
across the snowy plains except Cold Paws, a
bear so huge and so cold that if you touched
him, you would turn to ice.

But one day as Hannah was walking through the forest, she heard some beautiful music. She felt as if the gentle notes were stroking her ears.

That night as she closed her eyes, all Hannah could think of was the beautiful music. She knew she would have to follow it.

The next day, Hannah took the same path through the snow.

It led her out of the great forest, across the snowy plains,

Again she heard the magical music drawing her closer.

and right up to a large iceberg.

Hannah crept toward the iceberg
and peered around the corner.
Right there in front of her was a huge
polar bear with a soft, gentle smile.
He was playing a silver flute.

Hannah could not believe her eyes.
She crouched down out of sight
and listened until the air
fell silent around her.

"Brrrrrrrrrrrrrrrrrrrrrrr,"
the polar bear shivered. His whole
body shook, and the snow beneath
Hannah's boots trembled.

Hannah knew how miserable it was to feel very cold, so without thinking, she took off her scarf, stepped forward, and placed it right in front of the big polar bear.

Hannah held her breath.

Very slowly the polar bear picked up
the red woolly scarf and tied it under his big
furry chin. He nodded his large heavy head.

Hannah smiled.

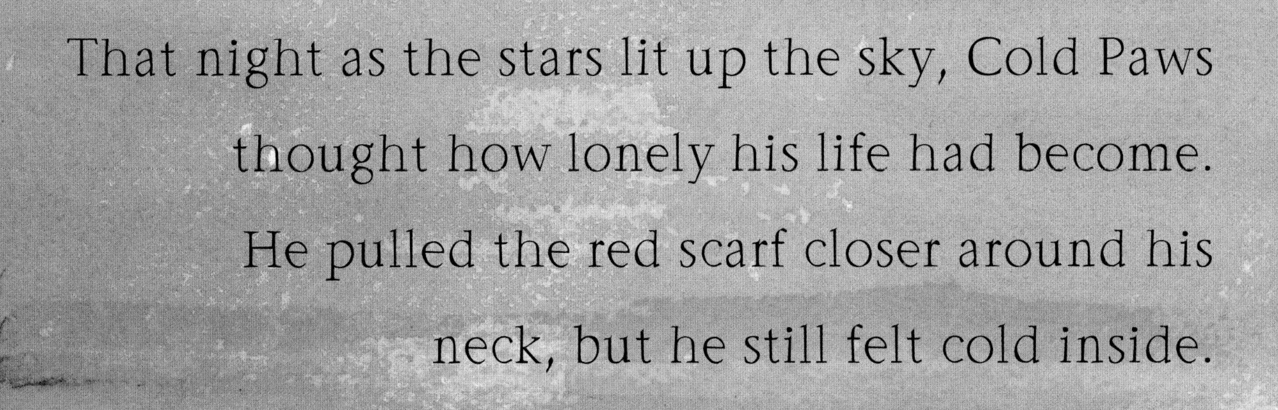

That night as the stars lit up the sky, Cold Paws thought how lonely his life had become. He pulled the red scarf closer around his neck, but he still felt cold inside.

"Brrrrrrrrrrrrrrrrrr," he shivered.

Back in the village, on the other side of the forest, Hannah lay in her warm bed and thought and thought about the cold polar bear.

The next day, Hannah ran back through the forest, across the snowy plains, and up to the iceberg.

"I have an idea. Let's do some jumping jacks to warm you up," she said.

Cold Paws looked confused and rubbed his ears. Something about the little girl made him feel better, so he lifted his heavy legs and did his best to jump up and down.

Hannah laughed and Cold Paws smiled.

"I have another idea," said Hannah, and she ran off toward the village.

As Cold Paws waited for Hannah to return, the sunlight faded and the snow fell steadily through the silence. He blew on his polar bear paws. Cold Paws had never had such a special day, but he still felt a little cold inside.

"Brrrrrrrr,"

he shivered.

When Hannah came back, she held out a steaming mug of hot chocolate. “This is for you,” she said.

Cold Paws took the mug in his soft paws and smelled the sweet drink. He took a large gulp and licked the chocolate off his nose.

He had never tasted anything so delicious, and now he felt only a tiny bit cold inside.

"I have to go home now," said Hannah.
"I don't know how to warm you up, but I'll be back to play with you every day."

Hannah gave Cold Paws a very big hug, and as she did so, a wonderful thing happened. The cold feeling inside Cold Paws disappeared and instead he felt a warm glow all over.

Now that he had a friend, Cold Paws didn't feel cold anymore.